Twelve Snails to One Lizard

A Tale of Mischief and Measurement

Twelve Snails to One Lizard

by Susan Hightower
pictures by Matt Novak

Simon & Schuster Books for Young Readers

SIMON & SCHUSTER BOOKS FOR YOUNG READERS
An imprint of Simon & Schuster Children's Publishing Division
1230 Avenue of the Americas, New York, New York 10020

Book design by Anahid Hamparian
The text for this book is set in 16-Point Berkley Old Style
The illustrations are rendered in acrylics

Printed in Hong Kong

10   9   8
Library of Congress Cataloging-in-Publication Data
Hightower, Susan (Susan M.)
Twelve snails to one lizard: a tale of mischief and measurement / by Susan Hightower;
pictures by Matt Novak.
p.   cm.
Summary: Bubba the bullfrog helps Milo the beaver to build a dam by explaining
to him the concepts of inches, feet, and yards.
ISBN 0-689-80452-0
[1. Measurement—Fiction. 2. Frogs—Fiction. 3. Beavers—Fiction.]
I. Novak, Matt, ill. II. Title.
PZ7.W668185Tw 1997
[E]—dc20 96-2403

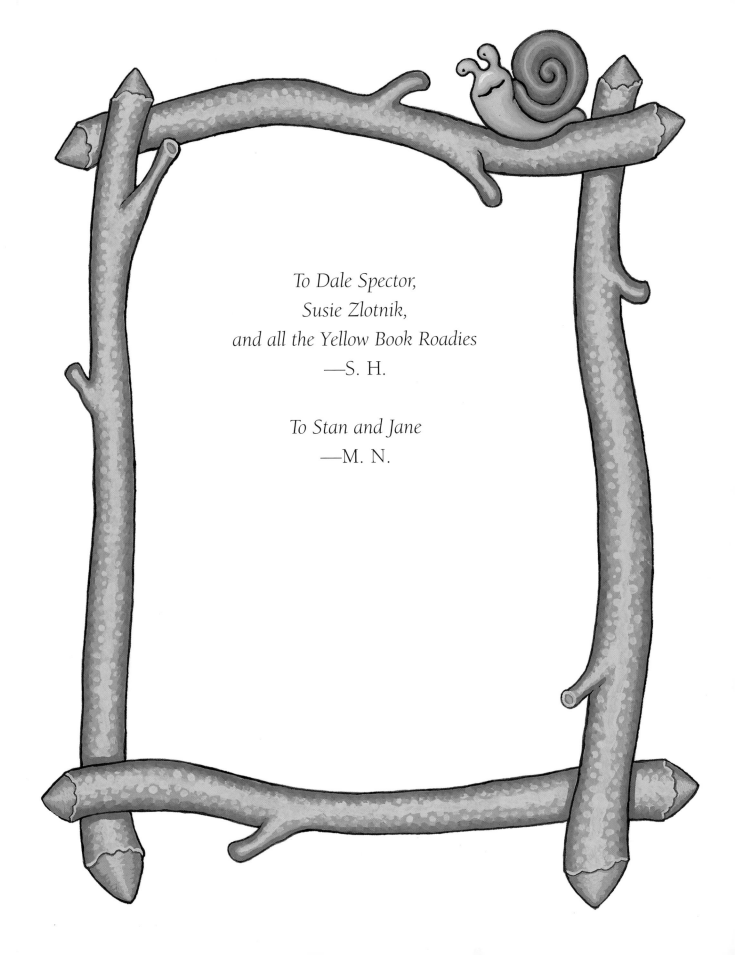

To Dale Spector,
Susie Zlotnik,
and all the Yellow Book Roadies
—S. H.

To Stan and Jane
—M. N.

"I sure do love to watch you work, Milo," drawled Bubba Bullfrog, as he sprawled back in the cool grass by the river bank. "In fact, there's nothing I like better on a warm day than watching a beaver work. I'd even give you a hand, but we bullfrogs don't have big strong teeth, or sharp claws, or nice flat tails like you do."

"You make a fine audience, Bubba," answered Milo Beaver, "but if I don't get some help with this branch soon, the pond may be dry by summer."

"What?" Bubba sat up. "The pond . . . dry?"

"Today is April first, and it's the last month of the rainy season," explained Milo. "If I don't get that dam fixed before the rain comes, all the rainwater will run off downstream and our little pond will be dry all summer."

"*Hmmm* . . . dry pond, no bugs. Wait a minute, Milo. I may not have strong teeth or a flat tail, but we bullfrogs are very smart fellows," boasted Bubba, "and I'd be happy to think about your problem for a while."

"Thinking isn't going to patch that hole in my dam, Bubba. I found a nice strong branch yesterday, but it was a bit too big so I took a little off each end. Then it was too small and it washed right through." Milo scratched his head. "I have to figure out a way to cut a branch so it will fit just right."

"You know," said Bubba, "my nephew's hopping class hopped that part of the creek just the other day, and their teacher told them it was exactly thirty-six inches."

"How long is an inch?" asked the beaver.

"Oh, I'd say an inch is about as long as a healthy snail," Bubba replied.

"One snail, you say? *Hmmm* . . . if one snail is as long as one inch, and I were to line up thirty-six snails, feelers to tails, they would measure thirty-six inches, right?"

"Sounds like quite a job, rounding up all those snails," Bubba answered, "but I believe thirty-six healthy snails, feelers to tails, would measure thirty-six inches."

"I don't know what I'm going to do, Bubba," sighed Milo, sitting down for a rest. "These snails are the slowest creatures on earth. They're happy to help, but by the time I get all thirty-six lined up, the rainy season will be gone."

Bubba leaned back. "Well, Milo, I seem to recall that twelve inches equals one foot, so thirty-six inches is the same as three feet."

"How long is a foot?" asked the beaver.

"Oh, I'd say a foot is about as long as one of the Iguana boys," answered Bubba.

"An iguana lizard, you say? If one young lizard is as long as one foot, and I were to line up three young lizards, nose to tail, they would measure three feet which is the same as thirty-six inches, right?"

"Lizards aren't slow like snails, and I do believe if you line up three lizards, nose to tail, they would measure three feet," Bubba replied.

"I don't know what I'm going to do, Bubba," panted Milo, plopping down for a rest. "These silly lizards won't hold still. The rainy season will come and go and I'll still be chasing them."

"Well, Milo," said Bubba, "it seems to me that thirty-six inches equals three feet and three feet is the same as one yard."

"How long is a yard?" asked the beaver.

"Oh, I'd say that a yard is about as long as Betty Jane Boa," answered Bubba.

"*Hmmm* . . . so if I could get Betty Jane to stretch out next to this branch I could measure one yard, which is the same as three feet, which is the same as thirty-six inches, right?"

"Snakes aren't slow like snails. Since there is only one of Betty Jane you don't have to worry about part of her running off and getting into trouble while you're lining up another part, and I do believe she measures very close to one yard."

"Bubba!" Milo whispered. "Betty Jane seems happy to help, but I sure don't like the way she's looking at me. How do I know Betty Jane measures a yard, anyway?"

"Well, Milo, I do believe that Betty Jane is one yard-long snake. In fact, I'll prove that I'm right. Wait here!"

"Here, Milo, this is a yardstick. It is exactly one yard long. Put it down next to Betty Jane and tell me if that isn't one yard-long snake."

"Wait just a minute, Bubba. You're telling me that this stick is exactly one yard long?"

"It sure is. See, it's divided into feet, there are three of them. It's also divided into inches, there are thirty-six of them. Yep, that's one yard, exactly!"

"You mean I didn't have to spend hours pushing those slimy snails into a line? I didn't have to run myself ragged trying to get those lizards to stand still? I didn't have to risk my life with that snake? I could have just used this piece of wood to measure thirty-six inches?"

"Say, that's right!" said Bubba Bullfrog with a grin. "I guess next time you'll want to borrow my yardstick!"

Some Measurement Facts
About the Animals in this Book

How slow are snails, really? A hearty snail can move about two and one-half feet in one minute. How long does it take you to move the same distance?

Common garden snails are often about one inch long. However, the African giant snail can grow to nearly sixteen inches, nose to tail.

Though most iguanas are pretty close to twelve inches long, some grow as long as six feet.

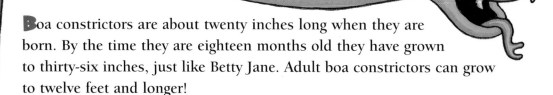

Boa constrictors are about twenty inches long when they are born. By the time they are eighteen months old they have grown to thirty-six inches, just like Betty Jane. Adult boa constrictors can grow to twelve feet and longer!

On the Jefferson River in Montana there is a beaver dam that is 2,140 feet long and strong enough for a man to walk across. In New Hampshire there is a beaver dam that is 4,000 feet long.

A fine, fit frog named Rosie the Ribeter holds the world's record for the longest frog jump. Rosie leaped 21 feet, 5 ¼ inches at the 1986 Calaveras County Fair and Jumping Frog Jubilee in California, shattering the previous record held by fellow frog, Weird Harold.